Bedtime for little Bears

Heather Maisner

Illustrated by

Tomislav Zlatic

W

FRANKLIN WATTS

LONDON • SYDNEY

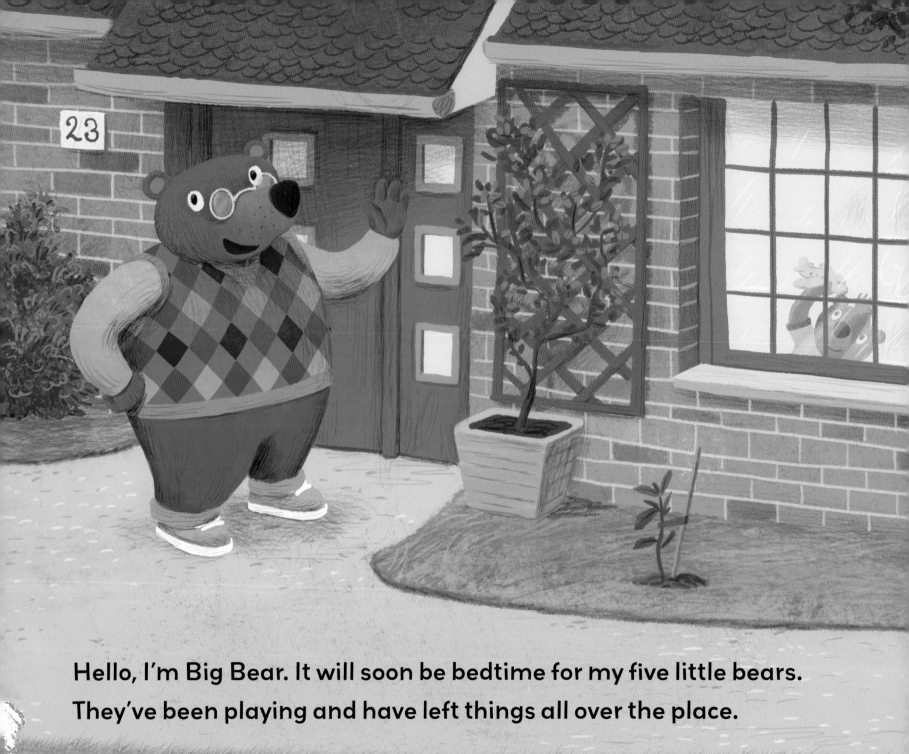

Hello, I'm Big Bear. It will soon be bedtime for my five little bears.
They've been playing and have left things all over the place.

Can you help me tidy up, please? And look for the cheeky little bears. They always hide at bedtime.

Fork

Jar

Plate

Just look at the kitchen! Someone has left things on the floor. Can you point to where they belong?

Cereal

Mug

Carrots

Eggs

Frying pan

Thank you. Did you hear that noise?

I think little Lily bear is hiding. Can you see her and can you find her red toy car?

Apples

Picture

Look at the living room!
Can you put these things
away, please?

Goldfish

Books

Newspaper

Cushion

Lampshade

That's better. Now can you find Jack bear and tell him it's nearly bedtime?

He'll want his toy aeroplane.
Can you see it anywhere?

Glove

Balls

Umbrella

Hello! Now we are in the hall. Let's put these things away.

Boot

Keys

Flowers

Coat

I think little Evie bear is hiding in here somewhere.

Where do you think she is? And can
you see her toy boat?

Flowerpots

Paintbrush

Bucket

The garage is a mess, too. Can you
help us put these things away?

Screwdriver

Spanner

Watering
can

Saw

Thank you. It's getting late now.

Where is Harry bear? I think he's hiding in here, and where is his green toy tractor?

Showercap

Here we are in the bathroom
and there are more things
to put away.

Toothbrush

Toilet roll

Towel

Duck

Flannel

Hairbrush

Well done. We've found Jack, Lily, Evie and Harry but we still have to find one more little bear.

Can you see Olivia bear? And where is her space rocket?

At last the little bears are ready for bed.

Can you put each bear into the right bed please, and give each one the right mug from my tray?

Goodnight, little bears. Now I can go downstairs and read my book.

Oh dear, where did I put my glasses?
Can you see them anywhere?

What a busy time we've had! Thank you for helping me.
I do hope you'll come and visit us again soon.

More from the Little Bears!

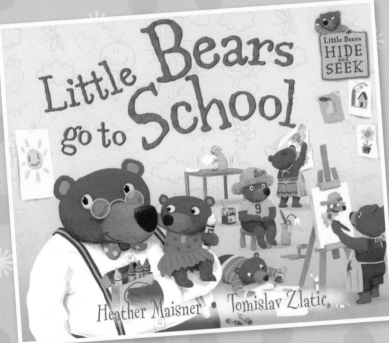

978 1 4451 4327 9

Little Bears go Shopping
978 1 4451 4325 5

Little Bears go on a Picnic
978 1 4451 4329 3

Franklin Watts
Published in paperback in Great Britain in 2019
by The Watts Publishing Group

Text copyright © Heather Maisner 2015
Illustrations © Tomislav Zlatic 2015

A version of this text was first published in 1988
by Walker Books Ltd.

Series Editor: Sarah Peutrill
Designer: Cathryn Gilbert
ISBN: 978 1 4451 4323 1
Library ebook ISBN: 978 1 4451 4193 0

Printed in China

Franklin Watts
An imprint of
Hachette Children's Group
Part of The Watts Publishing Group
Carmelite House
50 Victoria Embankment
London EC4Y 0DZ

An Hachette UK Company
www.hachette.co.uk

www.franklinwatts.co.uk

MIX
Paper from
responsible sources
FSC® C104740
FSC
www.fsc.org